For Jack.
You will never be too old for Mama kisses
or too big for Papa hugs. We love you!

Mama Kisses, Papa Hugs

Hardcover ISBN 978-0-525-65409-4
eBook ISBN 978-0-525-65410-0

Text copyright © 2020 by Lisa Tawn Bergren
Illustrations copyright © 2020 by Aleksandar Zolotić

Cover design by Kelly L. Howard; cover illustration by Aleksandar Zolotić

Published in the United States by WaterBrook, an imprint of Random House, a division of Penguin Random House LLC.

WaterBrook® and its deer colophon are registered trademarks of Penguin Random House LLC.

Library of Congress Cataloging-in-Publication Data
Names: Bergren, Lisa Tawn, author.
Title: Mama kisses, papa hugs / Lisa Tawn Bergren.
Description: First Edition. | Colorado Springs : WaterBrook, 2020.
Identifiers: LCCN 2019019880 | ISBN 9780525654094 (hardcover) | ISBN 9780525654100 (electronic)
Subjects: LCSH: God (Christianity)—Love—Juvenile literature. | Parent and child—Psychological aspects—Juvenile literature. | Love—Religious aspects—Christianity—Juvenile literature.
Classification: LCC BT140 .B457 2020 | DDC 242/.62—dc23
LC record available at https://lccn.loc.gov/2019019880

Printed in the United States of America
2020—First Edition

10 9 8 7 6 5 4 3 2 1

Special Sales
Most WaterBrook books are available at special quantity discounts when purchased in bulk by corporations, organizations, and special-interest groups. Custom imprinting or excerpting can also be done to fit special needs. For information, please email specialmarketscms@penguinrandomhouse.com.

Mama Kisses, Papa Hugs

by Lisa Tawn Bergren   art by Aleksandar Zolotić

Author of the Best-Selling God Gave Us Series

WATERBROOK

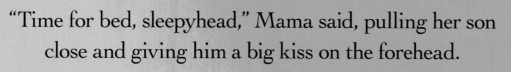

"Time for bed, sleepyhead," Mama said, pulling her son close and giving him a big kiss on the forehead.

He rolled his eyes. "Mama, I'm too old for kisses."

"Oh, kiddo, you are *never* too old for kisses."

"Never?"

"Never ever."

"What happens when I'm a hundred zillion years old?"

"When you are a hundred zillion years old, we'll be with God in heaven and he'll be showering us both with love."

"Kisses are good," she continued. "It's how mothers show our children how much we love them."

"Does every mother give mama kisses?"

"Well, I don't know about sloths," Mama said.
"Sloth kisses would be **very slow**. Like this,"
she said, leaning in for a long smooch on his cheek.

"Mama!" He laughed.

"What about lions? Or tigers?" he asked.

"Lions and tigers stick out their big pink tongues and give their cubs **_slurpy licks_**."

"Ewww. That's gross!"

"No, that's a special lion mama kiss. It's how
God made them. Want me to show you?"

The boy giggled and squirmed away when she tried.

"What if we were polar bears? How do they kiss?" he asked.

"If we were polar bears on our own little icebergs, I'd lean down and kiss you like this." Mama came close and **rubbed** the tip of her nose to his.

"That's **itchy**!"

"Well, it's a special polar bear mama kiss. It's how God made them."

"And you've seen how horses in the field kiss!
If I were a mare and you were a colt . . ."

"Oh no you don't!" He laughed, trying to edge away.

"Mama!" he cried as she **nuzzled** his neck. "That **tickles**!"

"Not to horses. It's how God made them."

"Mama, how does *God* kiss us?"

Mama smiled. "He kisses us hundreds of times a day. Although, if we don't pay attention, we might miss 'em. At night, he kisses us with a shooting star. In the morning, he kisses us with sunlight that crawls across the fields and streams into our windows. On a hot summer afternoon, he kisses us with a gentle breeze. But most of all, he kisses us through our family. That's how God made us to share love."

"So . . . what do you think? Since you're never too old for mama kisses, should we stick with *my* kisses or would you prefer lion or sloth or polar bear or horse kisses instead?"

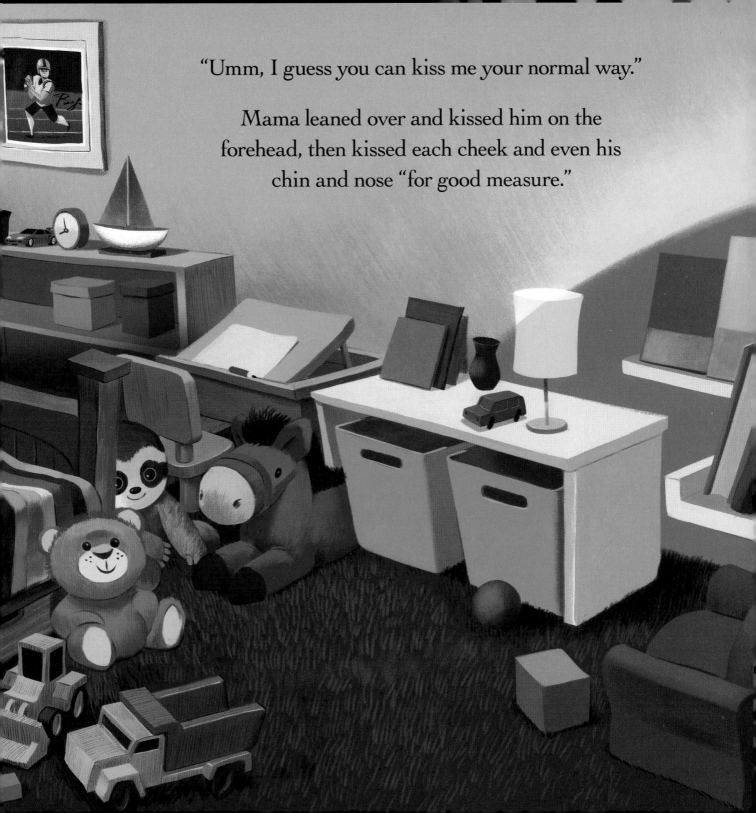

"Umm, I guess you can kiss me your normal way."

Mama leaned over and kissed him on the forehead, then kissed each cheek and even his chin and nose "for good measure."

And he even kissed her back.

Then Papa came in to say good night. They said a prayer together, and he leaned down and gave his son a big hug.

"Papa," the boy said, wriggling out of his arms. "I'm not too old for mama kisses, but I think I'm getting too big for papa hugs."

"Nah. You're never too big
for papa hugs."

"Never? Ever ever? What if I were as big as an elephant?"

"If you were as big as an elephant and I were your elephant papa, I'd **wrap** my long trunk around your head for a big elephant hug."

"That'd be weird!"

"It wouldn't be for us elephants. It'd be how God made us."

"What if I were a massive robot, as big as a building?"

"Then-I'd-be-a-mas-sive-ro-bot-too," Papa said in his best robot voice, "and-we'd-have-to-work-hard-on-it. But-I'd-still-give-you-a-pa-pa-hug."

He gave the boy a **STIFF, JERKY** hug that didn't feel comfy at all.

"What if I were a turtle? Turtles can't give hugs!"

"Sure they can. After a long day of swimming,
I'd have you, my little turtle, crawl up onto my back and
rest there, safe and sound. That's a turtle papa hug."

"That sounds **cold** and *shivery*."

"It'd feel good to us turtles. Because God would've made us that way."

"What if I were a stinky pig covered in mud?"

"We'd eat out of a trough," Papa said, snorting like a pig, "and roll in the mud all day, getting *super* stinky, and then we'd snuggle down at night together with the rest of our family in the pen. We'd be one muddy, slippery mass."

"That'd be icky."

"Nah. It'd feel right to us pigs. Because God would have made us for muddy snuggles."

"Papa, how does *God* give us hugs?"

"Hundreds of times throughout the day, God sends
us hugs. We might miss them if we don't pay attention.
He hugs us when we sing with others. Or when a
friend helps us. Or when snow blankets the hills
and everything is completely still," he whispered,
"quieter than we've ever heard before."

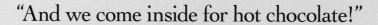

"And we come inside for hot chocolate!"

"Yes, hot chocolate! But most of all, God hugs us through our family. That's how he made us. That's why I give you papa hugs."

"So . . . what do you think? Should I start giving you elephant trunk hugs or cold, wet turtle hugs or ro-bot-ic hugs or muddy pig hugs?"

"Nah. God made you my human papa. I think we should stick with *your* kind of hugs."

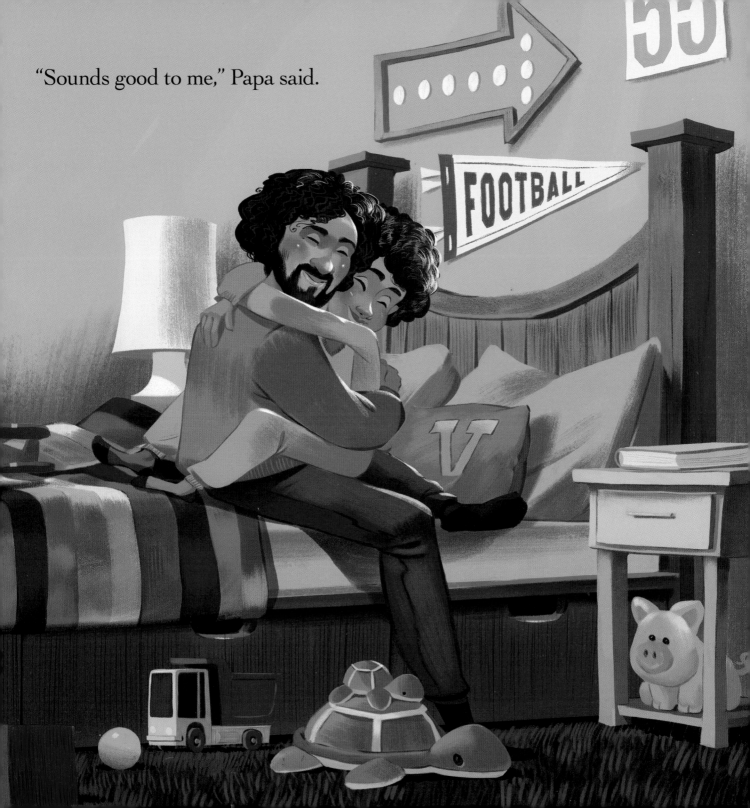

"Sounds good to me," Papa said.

Later that night, the boy thought about how good it felt to be loved so much by his parents . . . and how much more God loved him still.

And he knew, deep inside, he'd never be too old
for mama kisses or too big for papa hugs.

Never ever ever.